THE HIGH LINE

Preserving A Meadow in the Sky:
The Story of New York City's High Line

JULIE KNUTSON

Published in the United States of America by Cherry Lake Publishing Group
Ann Arbor, Michigan
www.cherrylakepublishing.com

Reading Adviser: Marla Conn, MS, Ed., Literacy specialist, Read-Ability, Inc.
Photo Credits: © Pit Stock/Shutterstock.com, cover, 1; © Dan Nguyen/Flickr.com, 5, 20; © Gagliardi
   Photography/Shutterstock.com, 6; © T photography/Shutterstock.com, 9; © Courtesy of Kalmbach Media,
   10; © Marianna Ianovska/Shutterstock.com, 14; © James Andrews1/Shutterstock.com, 17; © Brecht Bug/
   Shutterstock.com, 22; © Felix Lipov/Shutterstock.com, 23; © HildaWeges Photography/Shutterstock.com, 25;
   © Inspired By Maps/Shutterstock.com, 27; © Albachiaraa/Shutterstock.com, 28

Cherry Lake Press is an imprint of Cherry Lake Publishing Group.

Library of Congress Cataloging-in-Publication Data
Names: Knutson, Julie, author.
Title: The High Line / by Julie Knutson.
Description: Ann Arbor, Michigan : Cherry Lake Publishing, [2021]. | Series: Changing spaces | Includes index. |
   Audience: Grades 4-6 | Summary: "Learn more about how New York City's High Line park went from
   abandoned elevated railway to vibrant urban park and art space. Explore the logistics of repurposing the
   land and meet the people who made it happen. The book showcases a range of 21st century skills—from
   "Flexibility & Adaptation" to "Creativity & Innovation"—and shows how moving away from a tear-down
   culture towards one of reuse helps tackle a host of critical challenges facing our planet and population.
   Thought-provoking questions and hands-on activities encourage the development of critical life skills and
   social emotional growth. Books in this series include table of contents, glossary of key words, index, author
   biography, sidebars, and infographics"—Provided by publisher.
Identifiers: LCCN 2020006419 (print) | LCCN 2020006420 (ebook) | ISBN9781534168985 (hardcover) |
   ISBN 9781534170667 (paperback) | ISBN9781534172500 (pdf) | ISBN 9781534174344 (ebook)
Subjects: LCSH: High Line (New York, N.Y. : Park)—Juvenile literature. |Land use—Environmental aspects—
   New York (State)—New York—Juvenile literature.
Classification: LCC F128.65.H54 K59 2021 (print) | LCC F128.65.H54 (ebook) | DDC 974.7/1—dc23
LC record available at https://lccn.loc.gov/2020006419
LC ebook record available at https://lccn.loc.gov/2020006420

Cherry Lake Publishing Group would like to acknowledge the work of the Partnership for 21st Century Learning,
a Network of Battelle for Kids. Please visit http://www.battelleforkids.org/networks/p21 for more information.

Printed in the United States of America
Corporate Graphics

ABOUT THE AUTHOR

Julie Knutson is an author/educator fascinated by the endless ways in which people and communities can transform old spaces for new uses. She lives in Illinois with her husband, son, and extremely energetic border collie.

TABLE OF CONTENTS

Adaptive Reuse— More Than Meets the Eye

ESSENTIAL QUESTION: *What does an urban park built on an old rail line tell us about the past, present, and future of the city that surrounds it?*

It's an August evening in 1999. The place? New York City. Two strangers sit down next to each other in a space new to each of them: a community board meeting in the city's Chelsea neighborhood. Here—as elsewhere across Manhattan and its surrounding **boroughs**—residents sweat under a record-breaking heat wave. A previously unknown public health threat, the mosquito-borne West Nile virus, seizes newspaper and tabloid headlines.

Many saw the abandoned elevated freight track as an eyesore.

But that's not what's on the minds of these two community
members, Joshua David and Robert Hammond. Independently
of one another, they're there to participate in a dialogue. The
conversation centers on what to do with the neighborhood's
long-unused elevated railroad line. The two men are surprised
to find that most other attendees don't care about what happens

The High Line opened in 2014 and is now enjoyed
by tourists and New Yorkers alike.

to this 1.5-mile (2.4-kilometer) stretch of track. The others want
it torn down to make way for new development. Joshua and Robert
see things differently. They think it should be saved.

They don't manage to convince anyone else of their vision that
night. But they do exchange contact information. In the coming
months, they form a **nonprofit**, Friends of the High Line. They

build a **coalition** of supporters to save the towering metal structure and the 160 species of plants that have nested into this unlikely environment. They want to see it **adaptively reused** as a public park for the enjoyment of all New Yorkers.

Fast-forward 20 years: after a decades of work, the High Line stands as one of New York's most popular tourist attractions. Its gardens, cultural programs, and unique vantage points draw 5 million visitors a year. What does the story of this elevated urban park reveal about the city's history? And how is it used and enjoyed today?

The Curious Garden

Efforts to save the High Line and the plants and animals that thrived on it inspired author Peter Brown's 2009 picture book The Curious Garden. *In the story, a child named Liam nurtures the growth of a few scraggly plants along an abandoned rail line. In the process, he transforms his gray city into one bursting with color and life.*

Rail Lines and Cowboys on Death Avenue

Since its earliest days as a settlement, the island of Manhattan has been a place of goods and people in motion. The High Line's history is part of this evolving story of a city on the move. Two waterways connect Manhattan to the world beyond it. The East River, as its name suggests, runs along the east side of the island. The Hudson River flows along the west. For hundreds of years, commercial activity has bustled along the resource-rich banks of the Hudson. Its deepwater harbor drew settlers and traders, from Native Americans to Dutch colonists.

New York City's economy has always been supported by its waterways. In 2016, more than $90 billion worth of goods moved through the Port of New York.

One City, Five Boroughs

Manhattan is one of New York City's five boroughs. The others are the Bronx, Brooklyn, Queens, and Staten Island. Brooklyn has the highest population, and Queens is the largest in terms of land mass. While smallest in area, Manhattan squeezes more people into the space it has than any other borough.

New York City's west side was a global center of distribution, production, and manufacturing.

In the 19th century, the **Industrial Revolution** brought railroad transport to town. This new technology made it easier to **import** and **export** products not just across water but also overland. From 1867 on, cattle, produce, and supplies funneled into and out of the factories and warehouses of New York City's west side by way of steam-powered engines.

Birthplace of the Oreo

America's best-selling cookie, the Oreo, was created along the Hudson River Railroad's path. In 1912, the National Biscuit Company (now known as Nabisco) began manufacturing the crispy treat using incoming goods and resources. Rail cars then distributed these cookies from the Chelsea factory to the world beyond. Today, they can be found on grocery store shelves in over 100 countries.

Bustling freight lines ran at street level along the west side's main thoroughfares. This created a chaotic and dangerous tangle of traffic. In the 19th and early 20th centuries—all along 10th, 11th, and 12th Avenues—horse-drawn carriages and pushcarts wheeled alongside massive trains. Later, cars and bicycles jockeyed for space with these older forms of transit. The meeting of powerful trains with pedestrians led to dozens of unnecessary deaths: between 1898 and 1908, 198 people were killed in collisions along 10th Avenue. Often, the victims were children playing in the streets or along the tracks.

By 1908, more and more residents demanded safer streets and raised their voices against Death Avenue. The cause took on new urgency after 7-year-old Seth Low Hascamp was killed on his way to school in the fall of 1908. Five hundred of his classmates and peers marched in protest along 10th Avenue to plea for change. Rail companies responded by hiring cowboys to warn of oncoming trains. Mounted on horseback, these hired hands rode in front of the trains and waved red flags or lanterns to warn of their approach. This continued for many years.

West Side Cowboys

For more than 30 years, a posse of West Side Cowboys rode in front of the "Iron Horses" that barreled down 10th and 11th Avenues. Companies employed 12 cowboys at a time, recruiting these young men from the countryside and ranches. The riders warned pedestrians of oncoming trains and ensured that trains kept within speed limits.

The last rider trotted down 10th Avenue on March 29, 1941, at 10:50 a.m. Twenty-one-year-old George Hayde and his horse, Cyclone, led 14 freight cars loaded with oranges to their destination before hanging up their reins. After his career traveling up and down Manhattan's west side, Cyclone got a job at a riding academy.

Elevated freight lines made for safer streets,
but they were only used for 46 years.

Finally, in the 1920s, a safety plan was developed. Freight trains would be elevated 30 feet (9 meters) above street level. But it took a decade to make this a reality: it wasn't until 1934 that the above-ground railroad was ready for operations. The railway was purpose-built for cargo, zigzagging in and out of multistory factories and warehouses. Dairy, produce, and meat shuttled down its tracks, leading it to be labeled the "Life Line of New York." It didn't, however, last forever. The rise of superhighways and truck transport led to the decline and eventual demise of the rails. In November 1980, the last cargo shipment rolled down its tracks. It was three boxcars filled with Thanksgiving turkeys.

Looking up at the Possibilities

After that last turkey-stuffed train rolled down the tracks in 1980, nature slowly took root. Winds blew seeds onto the abandoned tracks. Birds on their migratory journeys dropped seeds along the elevated line. Some 160 varieties of native and non-native plants grew in this secret garden above the city.

Beneath the tracks, the neighborhood also changed. Auto repair shops buzzed at all hours. Inexpensive, off-the-grid real estate fueled the development of subcultures of all stripes. Artists and musicians looking for space to experiment found it in this part of the city that many chose to avoid.

This neighborhood on the west side of New York is known as Chelsea.

The Man Who Owned a Rail Line

In 1984, dance instructor, real estate consultant, and train buff Peter Obletz bought the High Line for $10. The company that owned it planned to demolish the rusting structure. But first, they had to offer it for sale to anyone who might operate train service on the unused line.

Obletz, who lived in two restored Pullman dining cars, seized the opportunity. His vision was to see trains again run along the tracks, delivering riders from Manhattan's west side all the way to Albany, the state capital.

Sometimes, people walking past looked up, wondering where the mysterious, metal **trestles** along 10th Avenue led. Some, like train buff Peter Obletz, even wandered on its tracks and dreamed up plans to bring it back to life. Others cursed the structure. They thought it should be torn down to make way for businesses and development. In the early 1990s, sections at the far south end of the line were demolished.

What Exactly is a Subculture?

Pokémon collectors, online gamers, graffiti taggers, and break dancers—at first glance, these groups might seem to have little in common. But they're all examples of subcultures. A subculture consists of individuals who form their own, unique "mini cultures," with their own sets of rules and behaviors, within broader society.

The wild space of the rail tracks attracted New Yorkers who were used to skyscrapers and sidewalks.

West Village resident Robert Hammond had long been curious about the metal relic that loomed over 10th Avenue. In 1999, he read a *New York Times* article about the High Line. The article noted that CSX Transportation, the owner of the rail, was open to reuse proposals. He also learned of an August community meeting to debate the structure's future. He went to the meeting to find out how he could participate in efforts to save it. As he and Joshua David—the only other advocate there for salvaging the High Line—found out, there weren't any.

So they launched a campaign called Friends of the High Line.

The duo knew that they'd have to convince the public that the High Line was a special place worth saving. Since not all New Yorkers could experience the off-limits, abandoned track, they brought in a photographer, Joel Sternfeld, to capture the unique landscape. After Joel's first visit to the site in March 2000, he requested one year to photograph the flora and fauna that had sprung up between tracks. Joel's gray-sky images had the intended effect: they exposed the raw beauty of natural, organic matter set against a backdrop of concrete and skyscrapers. People were intrigued, and others—from local business owners to city planners to celebrities—joined the effort.

The pair and their new allies battled on against those who thought that saving the structure was a waste of money. They presented the community with evidence of the economic benefits

Figuring out how to turn the industrial space into a thriving park was a problem that needed to be solved.

of adapting the structure into a public park. They researched and forecasted, concluding that any costs would be offset by tax revenue and increased property values. They presented this case to the new mayor's administration. In 2002, the city endorsed the project. Three years later, plans to undertake it were formally approved. A global design competition for the project was announced.

The competition drew 720 practical and not-so-practical entries from architects around the world—they all wanted a chance to transform this space.

A Public Space for an Ever-Changing City

The design and architecture firms selected for the project didn't incorporate roller coasters or artificial beaches or sky-high trampolines in their plans, as some of the more outlandish High Line proposals did. Instead, they aimed to preserve the magic and wildness of the "meadow in the sky." As landscape architect James Corner remembered, "The immediate feeling was, how do we not mess this up?" They *didn't* want it to be a commercial playground, where vendors sold soda and souvenirs. They *did* want the park to reference the history of the city around it and to provide visitors with new ways of being in and viewing their urban habitat.

New York's "meadow in the sky" features plants that are native to the area, easy to maintain, and resistant to environmental changes.

Corner's team—which consisted of the architecture firm Diller Scofidio + Renfro and garden designer Piet Oudlof—worked up a three-phase plan for the site. The first step to realizing their designs involved **remediation** of toxins and contaminants. The **viaduct** was stripped bare, and hazards like lead paint and asbestos were removed. A new drainage system was installed, and huge cranes brought in mounds of dirt for plant life and trees.

One of a Kind?

The High Line isn't the only park built along an abandoned rail line. In Paris, the Promenade Plantée debuted as the world's first elevated park in 1989. Inspired by the High Line, other U.S. cities, like Chicago and Philadelphia, have also converted old rail tracks to public spaces.

After 10 years of **lobbying**, fundraising, and planning, the first phase of the High Line opened in 2009. Phase two followed in 2011, phase three in 2014. The designers created a varied sensory experience along the 1.5-mile (2.4-km) path. There are amphitheaters and observation decks from which visitors can see and hear the

The High Line's unique features and designs make it one of the city's most popular parks.

Adapting forgotten spaces into useful places
can have innovative and beautiful results.

rush of traffic. There are decks and grassy lawns for leisurely lunches and lounging in the sun. There are stretches like the Falcone Flyover, where park-goers can inhale the scent of magnolia blossoms as they walk through a canopy of trees.

Sustainability on the High Line

From recycling food waste to offering compostable utensils to educating children about ecosystems, the High Line is a space that prioritizes **sustainability**. *Environmental outreach efforts extend beyond the rails. The Sustainable Gardens Project was recently launched to expand pollinator gardens across New York City.*

Like the city around it, the High Line is an organism that always changes. On any given visit, the experience shifts, influenced by factors like the weather, the plants in bloom, the people present, and the street life below. It's a place of movement—by rail in one era, by foot in another—that is, by its nature, suited to adaptation and evolution. But it's also a place with a history. From the rail ties that form the base of the paths to a signal light at Chelsea Passage at 17th Street, traces of the High Line's past remain. While not obvious, they're undoubtedly imprinted on the landscape. They live on, in a new form, in the structure itself.

Extend Your Learning

Much of the attention drawn to the High Line project resulted from the photography of Joel Sternfeld. Over the course of a year, Joel snapped images of the abandoned rail lines in all seasons. His photos, as some note, "fueled the vision of the entire preservation site."

Choose a place in your community to document in photos over the course of several months to a year. It could be your bus stop. It could be your school as students arrive in the morning or leave in the afternoon. It could be the exterior of your house.

What story do the photos tell? Who participates in making the place what it is? How does it change over time?

Make a photo book of your images and share your reflections on how the featured place is defined by the people who live in it and how it changes over time.

Glossary

adaptively reused (uh-DAP-tiv-lee ree-YOOZD) changed a structure from its original purpose to a new one

boroughs (BUR-ohz) one of the five political divisions of New York City

coalition (koh-uh-LISH-uhn) a group of people united around a common cause or issue

export (EK-sport) to send out products, goods, or services

import (IM-port) to bring in products, goods, or services

Industrial Revolution (in-DUHS-tree-uhl rev-uh-LOO-shuhn) large social and economic shift toward machine- and factory-produced goods

lobbying (LAH-bee-ing) trying to influence a politician or public official about a specific issue

nonprofit (nahn-PRAH-fit) an organization that serves the public good and does not exist to make profit

remediation (rih-mee-dee-AYE-shuhn) the act of fixing or remedying a problem

sustainability (suh-stay-nuh-BIL-ih-tee) done in a way that can be continued and that doesn't use up natural resources

trestles (TRES-uhlz) in architecture, horizontal beams supported by two pairs of sloping legs

viaduct (VYE-uh-duhkt) a long, elevated roadway or rail line

INDEX